MYSTERY AT THE CIRCUS

JOAN CANTRELL

Printed in the United States of America

ISBN 979-8-89114-085-1 (sc)
ISBN 979-8-89114-086-8 (hc)
ISBN 979-8-89114-087-5 (e)

Library of Congress Control Number: 2024910626

2024.10.25

MainSpring Books
5901 W. Century Blvd
Suite 750
Los Angeles, CA, US, 90045

www.mainspringbooks.com

CONTENTS

Circus!
LIVE
PLUS!

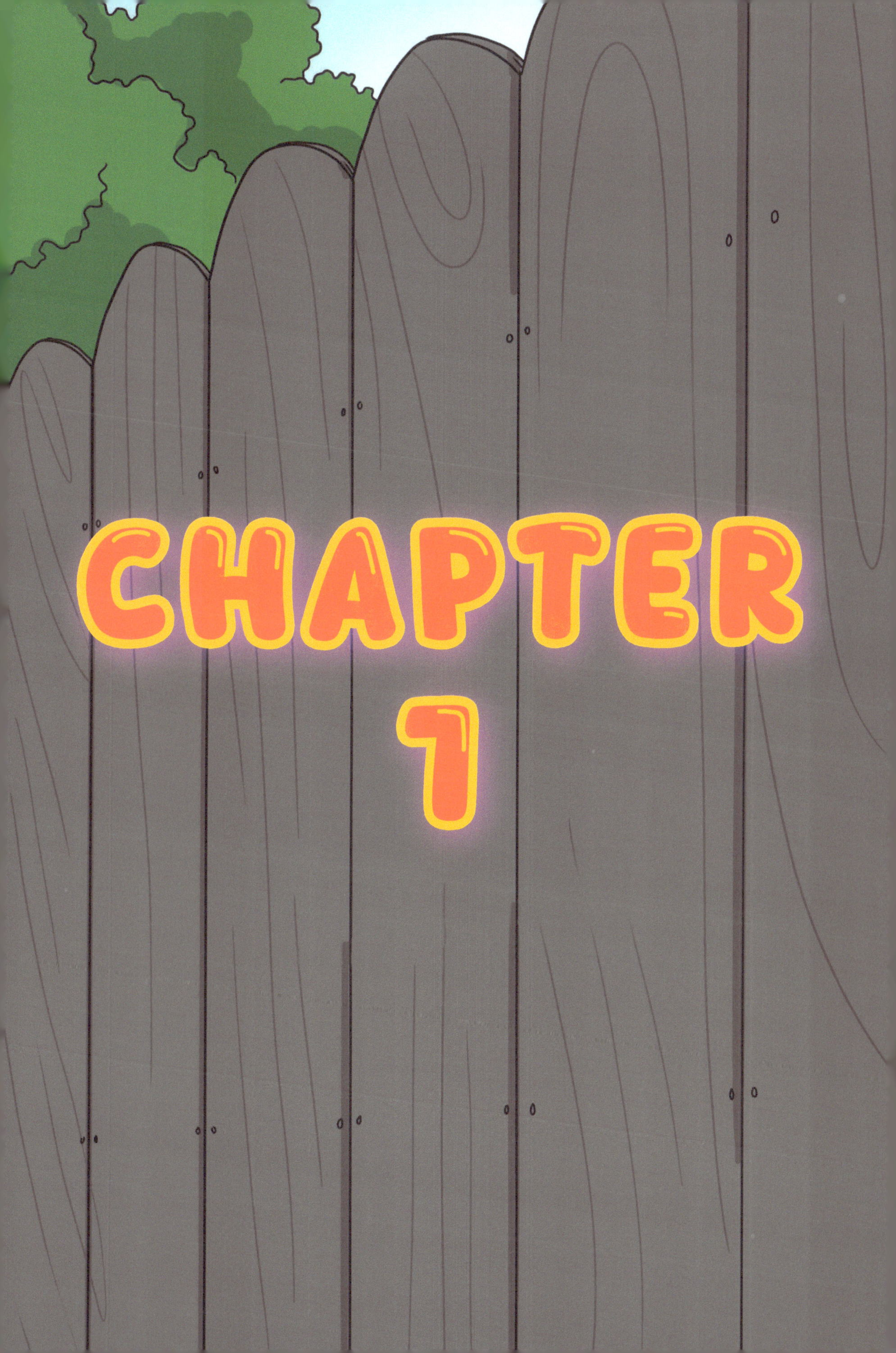

CHAPTER
1

oey walked down the sidewalk kicking a can as he whistled. He reached down to place the can in the direct line of the wooden fence to try to kick the can over it. There it was! Joey walked to the fence wide eyed and amazed by what he saw. There, in big letters on the poster: CIRCUS. As Joey read the poster, he became interested in the rare animal that the circus claimed to have. He just had to see it. He knew Amy, his sister, would go with him. She liked the same things he did. He took in the colorful poster with the clowns and umbrellas.

Joey raced down the sidewalk toward home. He flew in the front door and yelled, "AAAMMMMMYYYYYY!"

His mother appeared in the living room and asked, "What in the world is the matter with you? Why are you yelling?"

Where's Amy?" Joey asked as he tried to catch his breath. "I have to ask her something."

"Amy is at school. She won't be home for another half an hour. Now, Joey, what is this all about?" Mom's eyes narrowed as she looked at Joey.

"Well, the circus is coming to town. I want Amy to go with me. I saw a poster about it. It's going to be exciting. Can we go? Huh? Can we?'

Mom just looked at Joey. Then she said, "Sure, you can go. Now go to your room and get started on your homework before supper. I will tell Amy about the circus when she gets home. Scoot!"

Joey ran up the stairs two steps at a time. He opened his bedroom door and flung himself on the bed. He rolled over on his back and stared at the ceiling. Joey began to wonder about the rare animal the circus had. He just had to find out about it. He thought and thought. Joey sat up and reached into his backpack. He pulled out his math book "Yuck!" he said as he flipped to the page he was supposed to work on for tonight. Joey began to write down numbers and he tried to add them but he just couldn't think about math right now.

He thought he heard the front door slam. He ran to the top of the stairs and looked down just in time to see Amy toss her jacket on the chair. She disappeared into the kitchen. Joey went downstairs and opened the kitchen door. He saw his mom and Amy talking. Amy was crying. Her face was smudged and red. He quietly closed the door and went back up to his room.

MATH

CHAPTER
2

Joey finished his math homework, folded the paper and signed his name. As he was putting his book into his backpack, his bedroom door opened. There stood Amy looking as happy as always.

"What did you want? Mom said you had something to tell me." Amy waited for Joey to answer.

"Do you want to go to the circus? It's supposed to be exciting." As Joey was about to continue to convince his sister she starting sighing.

Oh, Joey. I don't know. That is such kid stuff. I don't think I'm interested in going to the circus with you." Amy turned and left closing the door behind her.

Joey just stood there. What has happened to Amy, he thought. Why has she changed overnight? Joey threw himself on to his bed once again and stared at the ceiling. That seemed to be the only thing he could think of doing at a time like this. He had to find a way to get Amy to go with him. He hadn't even told her about the rare animal the circus had. He bet that would do it!

Joey jumped up and opened his door. He ran down the hall to his sister's room. It sounded like she was crying again. Joey gently knocked on the door. "Amy, it's me. Can I come in."

Amy sat up and dried her eyes. She knew that she was going to have to tell Joey now. "Come in." As Joey opened the door, he saw his sister's face. It was red again. Her eyes looked funny. "What is wrong, Sis?" Joey asked, waiting for an answer.

"Oh nothing," Amy said. "What do you want?"

"I was wondering what happened to you today? Why are you crying?" Joey waited for an answer. Amy looked at him. "I had studied so hard for the big test in History. I didn't do as good as I had hoped." Joey sat there for a minute. "Do you get to take it again?"

"No." Amy replied. "The teacher said better luck next time."

Joey thought this would be a good time to tell her about the rare animal. "Well, I didn't tell you the best part about the circus. They have a rare animal. Don't you want to go with me to see it?"

"Yeah! Sure, Joey. I'll bet it's something made up and they are just calling it a rare animal. You know how circuses are." Amy turned to look out the window.

"Please, Amy. You have to go with me. Mom already said we could go." Joey knew if he pleaded long enough, she would say yes.

"Well, I don't know. When is the circus?"

Yes, he had done it. Amy was going with him. "Next week," Joey said. "The poster said the parade would be on Saturday afternoon at 2:00. We could go on Saturday night."

"Oh, ok!" said Amy

CHAPTER
3

Joey heard the sound of the drums as the parade began. Everyone was lined up on the sidewalk waiting to see the lions and tigers. Joey hoped for maybe a peek at the rare animal. He saw a covered cage on the back of the wagon. Nothing moved inside it. At least nothing that Joey could see. The crowd mumbled as the covered wagon passed by. Joey just had to know what was in there.

"Amy, do you think there really is a rare animal in the cage?" Joey looked up at his sister. "Who knows, Joey. "They might have something in there and they might not." Amy answered.

Amy and Joey stood and watched as the parade passed by. They walked home and ate. Mom didn't want them to fill up on junk at the circus. Mom gave them money to get in to the circus and some for treats Joey and Amy walked down the street to where the circus tent was set up and paid for tickets to see the show.

The tent was quickly filling up. Little babies were crying. Grandparents and grandchildren were trying to find the best seats. Joey saw the circus workers selling cotton candy.

"I want one," said Joey.

"One what?" Amy asked.

"Cotton candy," Joey said.

"Ok but that is all you get you know what Mom said," Amy liked acting like a grown-up.

Joey sat in his seat and pulled the cotton candy and touched it to his tongue. He liked the way it melted in his mouth. The band struck up a loud tune and the ringmaster began to announce the animals and their riders. Joey noticed that Amy was watching, too.

"Wow! Look at the size of that elephant!" yelled Joey.

"Look at the lions in the cages! I'll bet they are dangerous, "said Amy.

The brother and sister sat still and watched the circus. They watched the trapeze artists and the clowns. They laughed and laughed.

Soon Joey said, "Amy, I'm tired. Let's go home."

"Ok," said Amy. The two got up and left the tent.

Joey noticed the covered cage behind the tent. It was the same one he had seen in the parade earlier that day. "Hey, Amy. Let's go see that rare animal."

"What are you talking about?" Amy asked.

"There." Joey said as he walked toward the cage. "There is something in there."

"Wait! Joey don't go near that..."

"Oh wow!" said Joey

"Joey, what is it?" Amy asked.

Joey dropped the cage cover and walked away. He was mumbling. Amy chased after him. She kept asking him what he had seen.

"You wouldn't believe it even if I told you." Joey continued to walk toward home.

Now Amy wished she had looked too. She thought it would be hopeless to get Joey to talk. The two walked home in silence.

CHAPTER
4

"How did you two like the circus?" Mom wanted to know as Amy and Joey walked into the house. "It was fun, wasn't it, Joey?" Amy said as she punched her brother. They waited for Joey to answer. "What is wrong with him?" Mom asked.

"Beats me." answered Amy.

Joey walked up to his bedroom and got ready for bed. As he laid down, he thought to himself, did I really see it? Was it real or some made up animal like Amy said?

Joey was just about asleep when he heard the door open and Amy entered his room.

"Joey, are you asleep?" Amy asked.

"No, not yet. Why?" As if Joey didn't know what his sister wanted.

"Well, would you tell me what you saw in that cage? Was it really scary? What was it, Joey?" His sister was really interested and Joey was so sleepy.

Joey sat up in bed. He looked at Amy and took a deep breath. "Promise you won't tell anyone, especially Mom."

"Ok," Amy said. "Just tell me what you saw."

"A dinosaur." answered Joey.

"WHAT!!!" Amy yelled. "You're kidding, right?"

"No, I'm not. It had a long neck and a long tail. Its skin looked rough. Amy, it turned and looked at me. Did you hear me? I said it looked at me!"

"Oh, Joey. I can't believe it." Amy was amazed.

"Well, you better start believing because I know what I saw. I don't think it was a dressed-up animal." "Go to sleep. Get a good night's rest and we will decide what to do in the morning." Amy patted her brother on the shoulder and left the room.

The next morning Amy woke up and decided to check on Joey. He was already up and dressed. "What are you doing?" Amy asked Joey.

"Nothing. Just looking out the window. Amy, I wonder what they are going to do with a dinosaur? They didn't make it a part of the show.

Joey looked at Amy. It upset him when she didn't believe him. "Yes, I know what I saw. But I still can't figure out where it came from or how the circus got it."

The two sat side by side for a while. They stared out the window.

"Well, what do you say we go back down to the circus and see if the dinosaur is still there?"

Joey got up and Amy followed. The two walked down the sidewalk to the circus. They thought it was odd to be at the circus and no one was around. Joey looked toward the back of the tent where the cage had been and saw nothing.

"It's gone! Look Amy. The cage is gone. What could they have done with it?" Joey was stunned that the dinosaur cage was gone. His eyes searched the area around the tent. Nothing. Nothing to be seen.

"Hey, what are you two up to?" Amy and Joey jumped at the rough sound of the man's voice. "You two shouldn't be here. The show does not start until 3:00. Scat! Go home."

"Uh, sorry, sir. We were just looking around. We didn't mean any harm."

"Well, I didn't mean to scare you either. You know we have to be careful around here. With all this equipment and wild animals, the man said.

"Speaking of animals," Joey interrupted, "where is the covered cage I saw yesterday in the parade?" "Joey," Amy whispered.

"Oh, that. UM you don't need to know anything about that. That thing is dangerous. Now like I said, go home. Come back at 3:00."

With that the man disappeared into one of the tents, Joey went over to the tent and peeked inside, He turned to Amy. She could tell by the look on his face that he had found the dinosaur. "Come on, Joey. We had better go home like the man said, Let's go."

Joey stood still and turned toward the tent. "Come here, Amy. I want you to see this." Joey motioned for her to come and look in the tent.

Amy was scared. She tried to walk but her feet wouldn't move. She stood there and looked at Joey. "Well, Sis, are you coming or not?

Finally, Amy was able to move and she hurried toward Joey. She looked inside the tent just in time. The cage was being covered again. The big man who had told them to go home saw them. Joey and Amy raced for the sidewalk. They ran home,

When they got inside the house, they both leaned against the door. Amy asked Joey if he thought they had been seen.

"He who?" asked Mom.

Amy and Joey looked at each other. They knew they were in trouble now.

"Uh, we went, uh, we went to the circus," Joey said.

"Yeah, and uh, there was this man who told us to come back at 3:00." Amy offered.

"Well, what difference does it make if he saw you or not?" Mom had both hands on her hips and the children knew what that meant. No funny business. They had to tell the truth.

Joey thought he had better say something. So, he asked, "Mom, can we have more money to go to the circus."

"More money? What happened to the money I gave you last night? And by the way, what was wrong with you last night, anyway?" Boy, Mom was going to get to the bottom of this story and Joey knew she wouldn't believe it either.

"Too much candy," Amy blurted out.

"What?" Mom looked at both children and said, "Go in the living room and have a seat."

Amy and Joey looked at each other and took a deep breath. They sat in the living room waiting on Mom for her to come in and give them the third degree. Mom came into the living room and sat down. "Now tell me about the circus. Did you like it? You haven't mentioned anything about it.

Amy and Joey looked at each other relieved. "Well, Mom..." Joey began to tell her about the elephants and the tigers. Amy talked about the trapeze. The three of them spent the rest of the morning talking about the circus. At lunchtime Mom said, well, if you want to go back to the circus today, you two will need to eat,"

CHAPTER 5

The roar of the crowd could be heard on the street. Joey and Amy stood in line to get their tickets. As they stood there, Joey's eyes darted around the fair grounds. Where was the dinosaur? What had happened to it? If only Joey could get a picture of it then he could make everyone believe him. He knew not to talk about it until he had hard evidence that it really existed.

"Come on, Joey," coaxed Amy.

The two entered the stuffy, dark circus tent. As they made their way to their seats they talked excitedly about the circus.

Joey begged Amy for cotton candy but since she was in charge of the money, she wouldn't let him have any candy. Just like her, thought Joey.

Amy made a face. "Joey is that all you came for? To eat? Sit back and enjoy the show. And watch for..." Just then Amy saw the covered cage in the middle of the ring. "Look, Joey! Now we will find out if the dinosaur is for real."

The band struck up a lively tune. The spot lights moved all around the tent. The ringmaster strutted into the center ring. His voice boomed. "Ladies and gentlemen, I present to you the greatest show you will ever see. Tonight, we offer for your entertainment the rarest animal on earth." With a flourish of his arm, he pointed toward the covered cage. The crowd got quiet. The clowns began to lift the covering from the cage. Everyone was shocked because the cage was empty! The ringmaster stood there with a shocked look on his face. The clowns quickly covered the cage and rolled it out of the tent.

Everyone laughed because they thought it was a part of the show. Only Joey and Amy knew the real story. "Let's go," said Amy. "We need to check this out."

"Where could Doug be?" asked Joey.

"Doug? Who is Doug?" Amy wanted to know.

"The dinosaur! said Joey.

The children made their way to the aisle. Finally, they were outside the tent. They looked around. They found the covered cage. Joey and Amy raised the cover.

"What are you two doing? Get away from that cage." When Amy and Joey turned around the old guy said, "Oh, it's you two again. Look, I told you once to go away. Now leave or I'll call the cops. You understand? Now, git!

Amy and Joey walked slowly home. They wondered where the dinosaur was. "Maybe we can find him. If you were a dinosaur, where would you go, Amy? Joey questioned.

"Well, I don't know!" Amy said. "Why would I know anything about dinosaurs?"

The brother and sister walked home in silence. Thinking about the dinosaur, the two knew that the crowd had been wrong about the empty cage. They thought it was a joke. But Amy, Joey and the circus workers knew the real story.

CHAPTER
6

"How was the circus? The show any different than last night?" Mom was sitting in the living room reading when the two children entered the house.

Amy and Joey looked at each other. "Well, it was about the same," answered Joey.

"Yeah, I would say that, too." Amy responded. "Well, Amy said, "I need to do my homework." She went upstairs.

Joey heard her door close. He just stood there. "What is the matter, Joey?" Mom wanted to know. "Oh, nothing. I was just thinking about the circus." Joey walked over and sat down in the chair next to his mother. "Mom, Joey said. "Do you believe the circus could have a rare animal?"

"Rare? What do you mean?" Mom asked.

"Oh, I don't know," Joey said. He got up and went upstairs to Amy's room. He knocked on the door. "Amy, It's me. Can I come in?"

Quickly the door opened. Amy looked out and grabbed Joey and pulled him inside.

"What is the matter with you?" Joey said.

"Well," Said "Amy. I've been watching the circus guys outside my window. They seem to think the dinosaur is around here some place."

"What? Are you sure it's the circus workers? Let's go!" Joey ran out the door and bounded down the stairs and slammed the front door as he went. Amy was close behind.

CHAPTER
7

Joey and Amy stood in the yard and watched the circus workers. They were standing in a huddle talking. They seemed very sure that Doug was in the area. They had found his footprints. From what Amy and Joey could understand the workers thought he might be looking for his cage.

Joey shoved his hands into his pockets and looked down at the ground, thinking about Doug. As his eyes scanned, the grass he saw some odd-looking footprints near the bushes. His back stiffened. He shot Amy a look. The he looked down at the ground and then looked back at Amy.

She saw them too. She whispered to Joey, "Follow those prints."

She and Joey took off around the house. When they got to the backyard the children stopped in horror. They were standing face to face with Doug. He gave Joey a look of recognition. Joey and Amy realized that Doug wasn't a wild animal. He was tame. He was not going to hurt anybody. He was not dangerous like the circus worker had told them.

"Hi, boy," Joey said. He stood very still so as not to scare the dinosaur. "Looking for something?" "How are you doing, Doug?" Amy asked quietly.

The dinosaur looked at the boy and girl standing in front of him. He somehow knew that they were not going to hurt him. He nudged Joey.

"What are we going to do? How can we help him?" Joey asked Amy.

"Well, let's try to hide him in the basement." Amy opened the door to the basement. She coaxed Doug into the dark basement.

Joey quickly closed the door. "Now what?"

"Ok, what do dinosaurs eat?" Amy wondered out loud.

"First, I think we should probably get him some water. He is probably very thirsty." Joey went upstairs to the kitchen. He slowly opened the door and peeked into the house. He didn't see his mother anywhere. Joey found a large plastic bowl. He filled it with cool, clean water. He picked it up trying very hard not to slosh the contents onto the floor. He balanced the bowl of water as he made his way down the stairs.

When he got to the bottom, he gently set the bowl on the floor near the dinosaur. Joey reached out and patted him. "There you go, Doug. Drink up."

The brother and sister stood and watched as their new pet drained the water bowl dry. "Now what?" was all Amy could think to say.

"I know. Let's wait until after dinner. Then we will tell Mom we will clean up the dishes. Brilliant, huh, Joey?"

"Well, I don't think so. Mom is going to know that something is up if we volunteer to clean up the dishes."

"I guess you are right. We will have to sneak some food down later tonight. We can't let Doug starve." Amy sat on the cold concrete floor and watched the dinosaur lap up the water. "Joey, I'll get more water." She got up and reached for the bowl. Doug looked at her. "I'll be right back with more water, Doug." Amy said softly. She turned and tip toed up the stairs. She quickly opened the door and looked around the kitchen. Amy went to the sink and began to fill the large bowl again.

"What are you doing?" Amy heard her mother's voice behind her.

"Uh, getting water for a stray dog. He looked so pitiful." Amy said nervously. She left the kitchen carrying the bowl of water.

Back in the basement Amy watched as Joey talked to Doug. He stood close to the dinosaur and rubbed his hand on the animal's neck. They looked at each other. Amy thought that Joey and Doug looked like they had been best friends for years. It was like Doug had been there forever.

"Amy, we have to convince Mom that the stray dog is gone," said Joey. "We can't let her come down here. She will faint if she saw Doug. Boy, are we in big trouble."

Amy looked at her brother and said, "What are we supposed to do when we are at school?

We can't be her 24 hours a day keeping an eye on Doug.

The children heard the basement door open at the top of the stairs. "You two still down there?" They heard mom's steps on the stairs.

Both children raced up the stairs. "Yeah, mom. We gave the water to the dog and he is gone now," "Good job, kids. You know that if you feed and water him, he will be back every day wanting more. Remember, your puppy that you promised to take care of? I think I was the one who took care of him."

CHAPTER 8

The doorbell rang. Mom opened the door and saw the circus workers. "Can I help you?" Mom asked.

"Have you seen anything strange going on in the neighborhood today?" Asked the man.

"Strange? What do you mean? Mom wanted to know.

"Have you seen any strange animals?"

"Well. No. My children found a stray dog out back. Is that what you meant?" said Mom.

The circus worker raised his eye brows. Umm, could be. Where is the stray dog?"

Amy and Joey rushed to the door. "We don't know. We gave him some water and he left. He went back toward the circus tent," answered Joey.

There was another circus worker there. It was the man who had told the children to go home when they were snooping around the circus tent. "Hey", he said. "Aren't you two the kids I ran off the circus lot yesterday?"

Amy and Joey looked at each other. Then Mom said, "My children have told where your lost dog is. Is there anything else we can do for you?"

"Sorry, miss. We will be going now." Said the first man. The two circus workers walked down the sidewalk mumbling to each other.

Mom closed the door. She gave the two children a stern look. "What is this about being run off the circus grounds?" Mom patted her foot on the floor and waited for an answer.

Amy began, "Well, before the show began, we were looking around and this man came out and told us to leave. He said we didn't need to be there. So, we left."

Children, you know that I have warned you about talking to strangers. You were very lucky that all the man was doing was watching out for your safety. Please, don't do that again."

CHAPTER
9

CRASH! The children sat up in their beds. Joey ran to the door. He opened it just in time to see Amy running down the stairs. Joey raced after her. He knew where she was going.

Joey ran through the opened basement door. He heard Amy talking to Doug.

"Look at what you have done. Mom is going to kill us," Amy said angrily as she began to pick up the pieces of broken glass. "Well, do not just stand there, Joey, help me before Mom comes down here."

Joey found and old bucket and the two children began to place the sharp pieces of glass in it. The two worked quickly and silently. Soon the mess was cleaned up.

"Now what do we do? We are going to have to replace the window without Mom knowing it," Joey complained.

Amy stood silently. She was thinking. Then she said, "Well, can we help it if the stray dog came back looking for water?"

"Stray dog? Do you think Mom would believe us.?" asked Joey.

Just then they heard their mother coming down the stairs. "What is going on down here?"

"Nothing," said Joey. "It looks like the stray dog we gave water to came back for more.

"What did I tell You? You can't just take in strays." Mom went back to the kitchen. She got herself a drink of water and walked back to her bedroom. She laid down on the bed. She began to think about her children. They are so kind she thought. Giving water to a stray dog. Cleaning up the mess in the basement. Soon she was fast asleep.

The next morning Joey awoke to the smell of pancakes and bacon. That was his favorite Saturday breakfast. He quickly dressed and went into the kitchen hoping Mom had forgotten about last night. "Breakfast smells good, Mom. It woke me up."

"Well, I'm glad. You and Amy have a lot of explaining to do." Mom turned and faced Joey.

"I want to know what you two mean by keeping
a... Rriinngg. The phone stopped Mom. "Just a minute.
Mom picked up the phone and said, "Hello." She
listened intently. "I know. That is what I'm getting ready
to ask them about. Can I call you later, Alice?" As
Mom hung the phone up, she went back to the stove
and began flipping pancakes again. "What do you
two mean by keeping a stray dog in the basement? I
thought you said after you gave the dog some water
he left."

Amy and Joey looked at each other in disbelief.
They couldn't believe their mom still thought a dog
had caused all that noise last night. "I didn't see the
dog in the basement after we closed the door. He
must have slipped inside just as the door closed." Amy
waited for her mother to respond.

As soon as she poured the juice into Joey's glass,
he gulped it down. He set his glass on the table and
said, "More OJ, please" Mom refilled his glass and sat
down.

The family enjoyed their breakfast. They talked about what they intended to do with their day. Amy enjoyed Saturday morning breakfast. She liked the talk and laughter. Today the sunshine streamed into the little kitchen and she felt secure.

CRASH! BANG! Amy jerked back to reality with the sounds coming from the basement. "Darn. That dog he's back. Come on Joey. Let's go make sure he doesn't get into the basement again."

As they got up from the table, Joey turned over his chair. "Sorry, Mom. I'll be more careful next time." He followed Amy down the stairs. "Doug, you are going to have to be quieter. Mom is going to find out about you. Now stop it."

"Look," Amy said. something for him."

"Doug does not have much room to move around. We are going to have to do something.

The brother and sister looked at each other. They thought and thought. Finally, Amy said, "I've got it. We can take him out to the old barn on Grandpa's farm. No one will ever look there. He will have lots of room and we can fill buckets with food and water. We won't have to worry about Mom finding Doug and calling the circus. That way Doug will be safe."

"Brilliant, Sis. Doug will be safe. But how are we going to get him out to the farm?"

"That's easy. We will wait until late tonight and we'll walk him there. That will give us all day to get the barn ready." Amy felt so proud of herself. She couldn't believe she thought of a way to save a dinosaur.

CHAPTER
10

Amy made her way down the dark hall to Joey's room. He was sleeping She gently shook him. "Joey, wake up. We have to take Doug out to the farm. Come on...wake up."

Joey stirred under the covers. Then he remembered. The barn had barrels full of water and food for Doug. He and Amy had spent all afternoon cleaning out the barn for the dinosaur. Joey sat up on his elbows. "What time is it?"

"It's time to go. Let's get down stairs and move Doug to the farm before Mom finds out."

Amy, Joey and Doug walked in the moonlight toward the edge of town where their grandfather had once lived. The farm had been abandoned long ago. No one ever went there so they both knew that Doug was going to be ok.

As they neared the barn, Joey ran ahead and opened the swinging doors. Doug walked in and went into the stall where the food and water was waiting. "Ok, Doug, welcome to your new home."

Amy smiled because she knew that Doug was going to be ok and would not be mistreated by the circus workers. He was where he could roam freely and always have plenty of food, water and love.

"Come on, Sis. Let's go." Joey urged.

The children walked back home in silence, they were afraid someone would hear them. They enjoyed the crisp night air and looking at the stars.

"I wonder where the circus found Doug?" Amy wondered out loud. "You know that they just didn't find an animal and dress it up to look like a dinosaur.

"Maybe they found him in a jungle somewhere. You know how they say they have traveled the world looking for a new and exciting additions to the shows," offered Joey.

"I know," said Amy. "But they just can't explain where Doug came from."

The children neared their home. They found their way back upstairs to their warm beds. Both were fast asleep before Mom got up.

The house seemed quiet. Mom began to cook breakfast. She thought she heard something in the basement. As she opened the door, she saw a dog standing at the foot of the stairs.

"Amy...Joey... Get down here now!" yelled Mom

As Amy and Joey met in the hall upstairs, they both looked at each other and said, "Now what?' They knew it couldn't be Doug. He was safe at the farm. The circus workers would never find him there.

www.ingramcontent.com/pod-product-compliance
Lightning Source LLC
Chambersburg PA
CBHW041417300726
48978CB00003B/130